ONE COLD MARCH MORNING, little Grey Rabbit got up very early. Squirrel and Hare were both still sound asleep in their beds.

She took her basket and crept out of the house. The sun was not yet up and the stars were still in the sky.

Off she went, swinging her basket round her head.

Two startled mice peeped out from under the hedge. "I wonder where she's going," they said. "It's a pity she's lost her tail. They say it's fastened on Wise Owl's door!"

Little Grey Rabbit ran on until she came to a bank where the first primroses were growing. She bent down and started to put the delicate flowers in her basket.

Suddenly a pink nose poked up beside her.

"Oh! Moldy Warp! You made me jump!"

"What are you doing out so early?" he asked.

"I'm picking primroses for primrose wine. Hare has a bad cold."

How Little
Grey Rabbit Got
Back her Tail

BASED ON THE STORIES BY

Alison Uttley and *Margaret Tempest*

Collins

An imprint of HarperCollins*Publishers*

How Little Grey Rabbit Got Back Her Tail
was first published in 1930 by William Heinemann Ltd
This edition was first published in Great Britain by HarperCollins*Publishers* Ltd in 2000
Published by arrangement with Egmont Children's Books Ltd

1 3 5 7 9 10 8 6 4 2
ISBN: 0-00-710011-6

Text for this edition by Susan Dickinson based on the
television adaptation by Helen Cresswell
Text © The Alison Uttley Literary Property Trust 2000
Illustrations in this work derived from the television series © HTV LTD 2000
based on the original illustrations by Margaret Tempest.
Production of the television series by United Productions in association with Cosgrove Hall.

The HarperCollins website address is: www.**fire**and**water**.com

Printed and bound in Hong Kong

"Oh," said Moldy Warp. "But, Grey Rabbit, where is your tail?"

"I gave it to Wise Owl. He told me where to get carrot seed."

"Oh, he did, did he? Grey Rabbit, would you like your tail back very much?"

"Yes I would, very, very much," she sighed.

"I'll help you, Grey Rabbit. I'll think of a plan."

"Oh, thank you, Moldy Warp."

When Squirrel and Hare got up, they couldn't find Grey Rabbit anywhere.

"Where are you, Grey Rabbit?" they called. "Are you hiding?"

"Achoo! Achoo!" sneezed Hare.

"Her basket has gone. She must have gone out!" said  Squirrel. "I suppose *we* had better get the breakfast."

"Achoo!" sneezed Hare again. He seized the tablecloth and wrapped it around his shoulders.

"Oh, do be careful!" cried Squirrel.

She tried to grab the tablecloth from Hare, but at
that moment the door opened and in stepped little
Grey Rabbit.

"Hare, Squirrel! Look at my
primroses, picked with the dew
still on them. Now we can make
primrose wine to cure your
cold, Hare."

All day long they made the wine. Little Grey Rabbit put the primrose flowers in layers in a wooden cask and between each layer she put an acorn cup of honey and a squeeze of wood sorrel juice. Squirrel ran to the brook many times to fill the kettle.

When the water was boiling Grey Rabbit poured it over the flowers until the cask was full. Then she sealed it with melted beeswax and they buried it in the garden.

"When can I have some?" said Hare as they sat down to tea.

"In twenty-four hours," said little Grey Rabbit.

"I shall start counting now," said Hare.

That night Wise Owl flew over the house.

"Too-whit-a-tishoo, too-wishooo!" came floating on the wind.

Little Grey Rabbit heard him from her bedroom window.

"Oh, poor Wise Owl. He has a cold too. I must take him a bottle of primrose wine."

The next day Hare stayed in bed with a hanky tied round his head, playing noughts and crosses.

Little Grey Rabbit sat by the fire mending her apron. Squirrel was in the garden, pulling carrots. When she came in, she was cold and cross.

"It's bitter today, Grey Rabbit. And look at my tail! Where's my teasel brush?"

"Now stand still and I'll brush it for you," said little Grey Rabbit.

"Oh, that teasel's all worn!" cried Squirrel.

"Don't worry," said Grey Rabbit. "I'll get you another one."

And off she went to the teasel field.

"Hah! I've won again," shouted Hare. "I'm champion at noughts and crosses."

"Of course you always win, if you play against yourself!" snapped Squirrel. "Anyway, here's Grey Rabbit back again," she said. "Did you get my teasel?"

"Of course I did," said little Grey Rabbit.

"Now it must be time for the wine!" shouted Hare.

"Yes," said Grey Rabbit. "I think it is."

So they dug up the cask. When the seals were broken, a delicious smell came into the room. They filled their glasses with the golden wine.

"Mmmm," said Hare. "I feel better already."

Then little Grey Rabbit filled a bottle and tucked it under her arm to take to Wise Owl.

It was a dark night and the wood was full of little sounds, rustles and murmurs. Little Grey Rabbit felt very frightened for they were not comfortable sounds.

"Too-wishoo! Too-wit-ashoo!" came through the trees. Little Grey Rabbit looked up. There were Wise Owl's eyes shining in the dark. And beside his front door was her own white tail!

"A truce, Wise Owl," she said. "I've brought you a bottle of primrose wine for your sneezes."

"Thank you, Grey Rabbit. What would you like in – Ashoo – in exchange?"

Little Grey Rabbit looked at her sad little tail hanging there.

Wise Owl saw her look.

"No. I couldn't part with that," he said.

"Not unless you bring me a bell to go ting-a-ling when visitors call."

"But, Wise Owl, where shall I find a bell?"

"The world is full of bells," said Wise Owl, and he flew off.

When little Grey Rabbit reached home, Squirrel and Hare were waiting for her.

"Here she comes! She's here!" they cried. "Look what Moldy Warp has brought you!"

"It's a Roman penny," said Moldy Warp. "I found it deep down in the earth. I thought it would do for Wise Owl's door knocker."

"Oh, Moldy Warp, how kind you are. But Wise Owl will only give me back my tail in exchange for a bell."

"A bell? Where can we get a bell?" wondered Moldy Warp.

"A bell rings people to church," said Hare.

"There's a bell in the village shop," remembered little Grey Rabbit.

"There are harebells, bluebells and Canterbury bells," said Squirrel.

"I might make a bell," said Moldy Warp suddenly.

And he got down off his chair and went out, talking
to himself.

"I'm going to the village shop to get
that bell!" announced Squirrel.

"Oh, Squirrel! Please don't!"
cried little Grey Rabbit.

But Squirrel had gone.

She ran to the village, and followed a woman into the shop. The bell gave a loud ting-a-ling when the door was opened.

Up Squirrel sprang and landed on the bell which jangled loudly as it swung to and fro.

She bit and tugged and pushed, and at last the bell, with Squirrel still hanging on to it, fell to the floor, knocking over a bowl of eggs on the way.

The two women ran screaming from the shop.

Away ran Squirrel, pulling the jingling, jangling bell behind her, through the village and home.

"Oh, how clever you are!" cried Grey Rabbit.

Then little Grey Rabbit and Hare dragged the bell through the wood to Wise Owl's house. He put out his head with half-shut eyes and hooted.

"Who's making all that hullabaloo?" he called. "How can I sleep with that jingle jangle?"

"But we've brought you a…" said Hare.

"Take it away!" And Wise Owl slammed his door behind him.

So little Grey Rabbit and Hare left the bell in the wood and went sadly home.

There they found Squirrel talking to Moldy Warp.

"Hare! Grey Rabbit! Look what Moldy Warp has made from that old silver coin!" she cried excitedly. "Ring it for them, Moldy Warp."

When Moldy Warp
shook the little bell a
sweet silvery ting-a-ling
came from it, so thin
and so musical that
little Grey Rabbit
looked out to see if the
stars were singing.

Then Grey Rabbit
started off with it in the
dusk to Wise Owl's
house.

As she carried the little
bell through the wood
she felt no fear, and the
whole wood held its
breath to listen.

Wise Owl's door was shut fast, but little Grey Rabbit tinkled the little silver bell softly.

The door opened. "What is that?" asked Wise Owl, peering down at her from his big oak tree.

"A truce, Wise Owl. A bell for my tail."

"You can have your tail, Grey Rabbit. Give me the bell."

Wise Owl rang the little bell gently.

"It is soft, it is beautiful, it is wise, for it lived in the beginning of the world," he murmured.

He hung the bell beside his front door. And he gave little Grey Rabbit back her tail in exchange.

When she got home everyone said it was as good as ever!

Moldy Warp smiled and took with him to his house under the green fields a bottle of little Grey Rabbit's primrose wine and the thanks of them all.